Really Easy Guitar!

How to read TAB

T0071321

PLAYBACK+
Speed • Pitch • Balance • Loop

To access audio visit:
www.halleonard.com/mylibrary

2288-2307-4892-8256

Contents

World headquarters, contact:
Hal Leonard
7777 West Bluemound Road
Milwaukee, WI 53213
Email: info@halleonard.com

In Europe, contact:
Hal Leonard Europe Limited
42 Wigmore Street
Marylebone, London, W1U 2RY
Email: info@halleonardeurope.com

In Australia, contact:
Hal Leonard Australia Pty. Ltd.
4 Lentara Court
Cheltenham, Victoria, 3192 Australia
Email: info@halleonard.com.au

Order No. AM981607
ISBN 1-84609-316-3
This book © Copyright 2005 Wise Publications

No part of this publication may be reproduced in
any form or by any means without the prior written
permission of the Publisher.

Visit Hal Leonard Online at
www.halleonard.com

Written and arranged by Nick Minnion
Music processed by Paul Ewers
Edited by David Harrison
Cover and book design by Chloë Alexander
Cover and artist photographs courtesy of
London Features International
Other photographs by George Taylor

▼Katie Melua

Introduction

Welcome to *Really Easy Guitar! How to read TAB*.

This book shows you how each element of guitar playing is represented in guitar tablature — also known as TAB. It also offers handy tips and advice on how to improve your TAB reading.

For each new element introduced, the book uses photos and diagrams, together with backing tracks to demonstrate how it should be played.

To help you apply what you learn, sample tabs of guitar riffs, licks, solos and rhythm parts in a variety of popular styles are included with corresponding sample and backing tracks to accompany you.

At the end of the book there is an instant look-up chart of all the tab elements, for ready reference.

Just take one step at a time. And have fun!

Tune Your Guitar

1 Before you can start to play along with the backing tracks, you'll need to make sure that your guitar is in tune . Track 1 gives you notes to tune to for each string, starting with the top E string, and then working downwards.

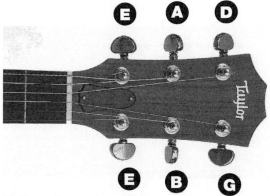

Alternatively, tune the bottom string first and then tune all the other strings to it.

Follow the tuning diagram below and tune from the bottom string upwards.

6th to 5th string	5th to 4th string	4th to 3rd string	3rd to 2nd string	2nd to 1st string

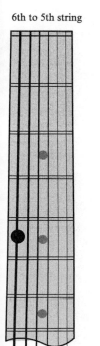 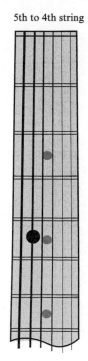 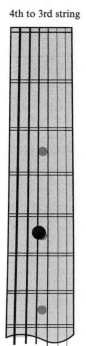  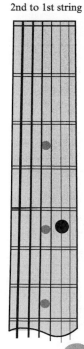

Understanding fretbox diagrams

Throughout this book, fretbox diagrams are used to show chord shapes and scale patterns. Think of the box as a view of the fretboard from head on – the thickest (lowest) string is on the left and the thinnest (highest) string is on the left.

The horizontal lines correspond to the frets on your guitar; the circles indicate where you should place your fingers.

An x above the box indicates that the string should not be played; an o indicates that the string should be played open.

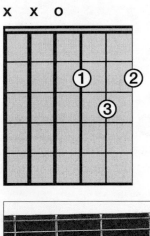

So, when you're playing this chord of D, make sure that you don't hit the bottom two strings.

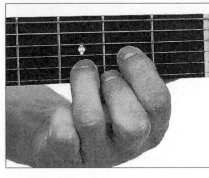

All the chords you need for each song are given at the top of the song, in the order that they appear in that song.

Shapes that are played higher up the neck are described in the same way – the lowest fret used is indicated to the left of the box. A curved line above the box shows that a first finger barre should be used.

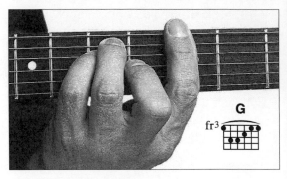

This barre chord of G is played at the third fret, with the first finger stretching across all six strings.

Am

Am/G

D9/F#

F

4

Lines and fret numbers

Tab uses six horizontal lines to represent each of the six strings on the guitar.

The line at the top is the first string (highest sounding):

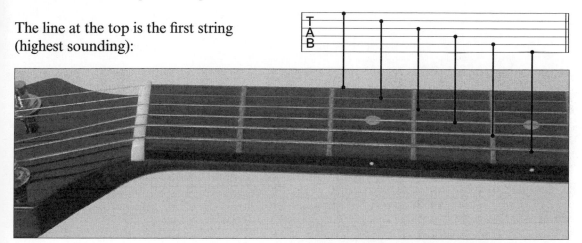

Each note is represented by a number positioned on a line.

The number tells you which fret to place your finger on.

The line tells you which string the note is on. A zero (0) placed on a line means you play the string open:

TAB is read from left to right, meaning that you play each note as you come to it.

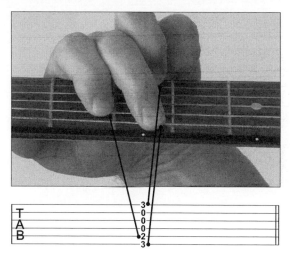

Repeat signs

A repeat sign looks like this:

When you come to this sign you scan back through the TAB, looking for the last repeat sign facing the other way (a 'Repeat from' sign):

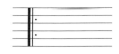 If there is no 'Repeat from' sign, you repeat the tab from the beginning.

Warm-up exercises

HERE"ARE"A"FEW" tab-reading exercises to get you started.
Listen to the tracks first to get an idea of how each tune should sound, then give it a go!

Once you are up to speed with each tab, try playing along with the track.

2 Getting A Grip

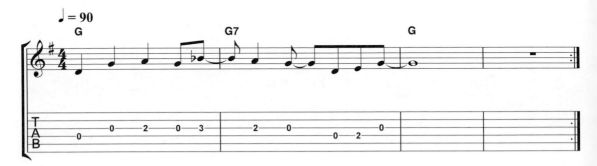

3 Simple Saints

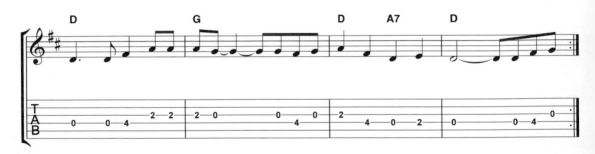

4 Smokin' In The Bathroom

Slow and heavy ♩ = 80

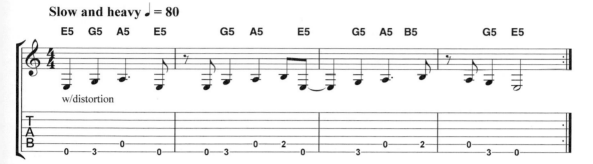

5 Rock Away The Blues

♩ = 100

Basic Left Hand Techniques

Basic Left Hand* Techniques

*If you play guitar left handed then your left hand is the one at the end of your right arm!

6   The Hammer-On

PICK A STRING once and then add an extra note by 'hammering' a left hand finger onto the same string at a higher fret.
A hammer-on is shown by a slur sign (⌢).

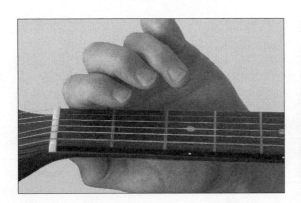

Here's a practice piece to get you used to reading hammer-ons:

7   Hammering It Home

♩ = 80

Some tab systems use the letters 'H' or 'HO' to show a hammer-on,
and 'P' or 'PO' to show a pull-off.

10

8 The Pull-Off

PICK A FRETTED string once and then add an extra note by lifting the finger off the string to allow the lower note to sound. A pull-off is also shown by a slur sign (⌒).

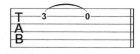

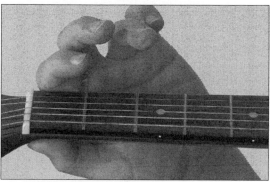

If a slur sign is used on its own, it is still easy to tell the difference between hammer-ons and pull-offs: for a hammer-on, the second note will be at a higher fret than the first; for a pull-off the second note will be at a lower fret. Try this:

9 On The Pull

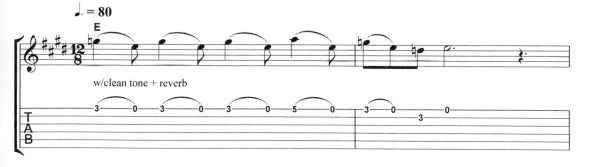

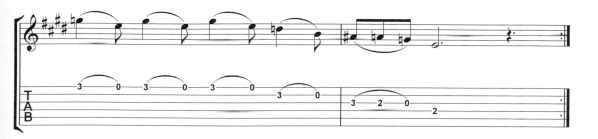

10 The Slide

A SHORT, STRAIGHT line linking two notes on the tab means you play
the first note, slide your finger up or down the fretboard to the
second note and then play that note by striking the same string again.

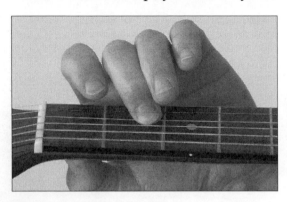

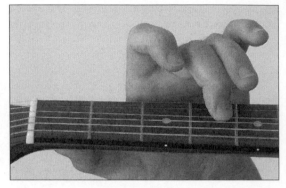

The legato slide

IF THE TWO notes are also connected by a slur sign (⌢)
the phrase is played as a legato slide.
This means that that the string is struck only once.

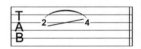

Decorative slide

A SLIDE IS often used to add an effect to a note.
In this case, the exact length of slide is not important
so it is left unspecified on the TAB:

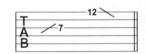

Tip#2

Slipping and sliding

The exact speed of a slide cannot be shown with tab.

So it is important to listen carefully and practice the phrase until it sounds
just right. Some slides are so fleeting you barely hear the first note;
others linger on the first note and barely touch the second.

Trust your ears!

11 Minor Slide

HERE'S AN EXAMPLE using lots of legato slides:

▼ **Keith Richards**

Chords

A CHORD IS HEARD when two or more notes in harmony with each other are played at the same time. On TAB this shows up as a vertical line of notes piled one on top of another. At first glance chords can look a bit confusing in TAB, but read on and see if we can simplify things a bit:

Here are some commonly used chords shown in both fretbox and TAB form:

G

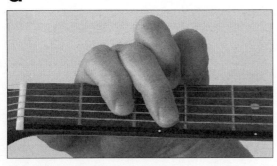

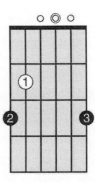

D

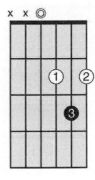

Am

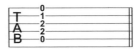
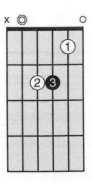

12 Shaping Up In G

TRY STRUMMING through this song. It uses the familiar chord shapes for G, D, Em and C:

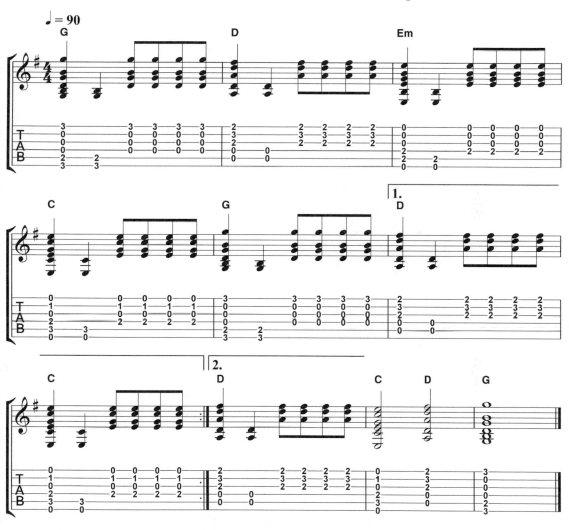

Keeping in shape

Tip#3

When you see a pile of numbers on top of each other don't try to figure out each individual finger as a single note.

Try, instead, to 'see the shape' that the numbers make. This takes a bit of practice, but will speed up your tab reading considerably.

Arpeggiated chords

WHEN YOU PLAY a chord one note at a time, instead of strumming the notes all at once, you are playing an arpeggio.

Arpeggios are usually played ascending and descending which shows up on TAB as a wave-like pattern:

13 Am

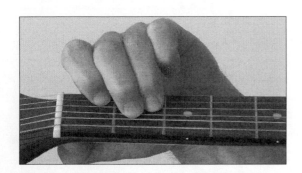 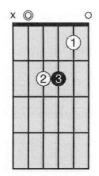

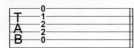

▲ Strummed

▲ Arpeggiated

Tip #4

Seeing the whole picture

Look out for the characteristic 'wave-shape' of an arpeggio.

Then try to spot the chord shape behind the pattern of notes.

It's usually then just a case of holding down the shape while you pick the strings in ascending and then descending order.

14 House Of The Rising Sun *(Traditional. arr. N. Minnion)*

TRY TO SPOT the chord shape on the following traditional song:

▼ Bob Dylan

Ornamented chords

MANY SONGS USE common chords with notes added to them in a repeated pattern to make a more intricate accompaniment.

Here's an example of adding a D note to a C major chord.
Technically, this forms a new chord named C added ninth or Cadd9:

Cadd9

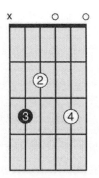

▼ Ritchie Sambora

Look before you leap

When reading a piece of TAB for the first time, rather than just playing each note as it appears, look ahead at the whole bar.

Very often the notes in each bar will mostly belong to just one chord shape, perhaps with a couple of added notes here and there.

Once again, by 'seeing the shape' behind the numbers, your TAB reading will be made quicker and easier.

Tip #5

15 Added Attraction

PRACTICE 'SEEING THE SHAPE' on the following piece:

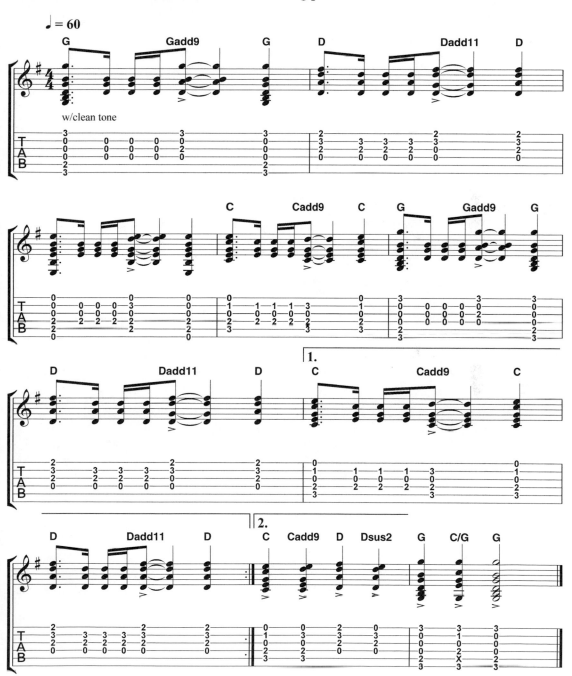

Basic Left Hand Techniques

Power chords

SINCE THE START of the 1990s there has been a proliferation of songs written using only power chords.

The term 'power chord' refers to a chord with just two different notes – the first and fifth in the key. They are written as '5th' chords (eg. C5, G5, E♭5...). Often, the first (*or root*) note is repeated an octave higher to make a fuller sounding, 3-note power chord.

16 F5 Power Chord

▲ **Two-note shape**

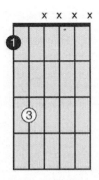

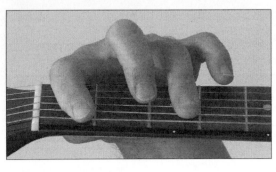

▲ **Three-note shape**

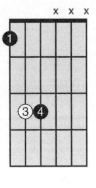

▶ **Dave Navarro**

20

B♭5 Power Chord

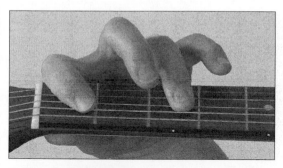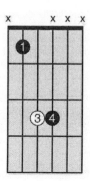

▲ Two-note shape

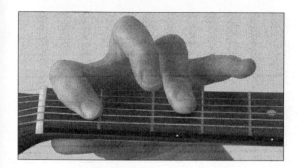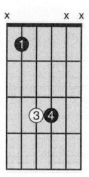

▲ Three-note shape

```
T
A----3----3----3----3-------3----3----3----3---
B----3----3----3----3-------3----3----3----3---
-----1----1----1----1-------1----1----1----1---
```

Tip #6

Getting to the bottom of power chords

Power chords are pretty easy to spot in TAB.

The fret numbers are typically two steps apart (ie. 2 and 4 or 3 and 5)
and on adjacent strings.

In each case, once you have looked ahead and spotted that
a bunch of power chords are coming up, you need only read the
lower of the two fret numbers for each chord, to position the shape
in the right place.

Basic Left Hand Techniques

17   Classic Rock Crazy

TRY LOOKING AHEAD for power chords with these songs:

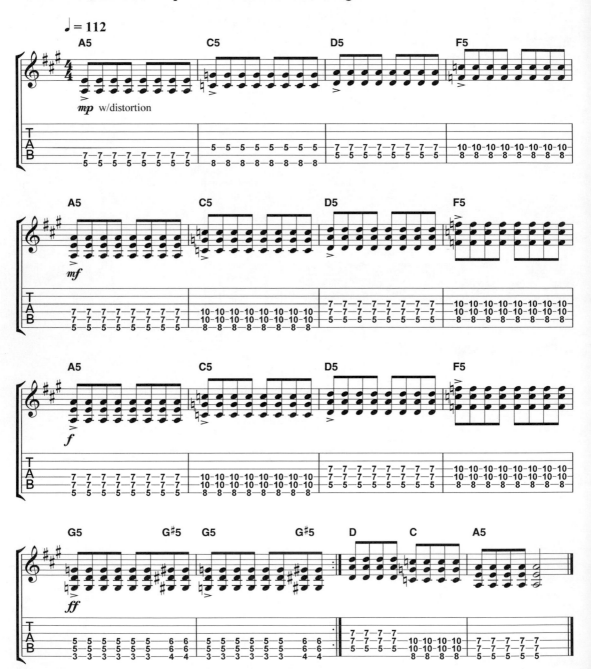

18 The Great Grunge

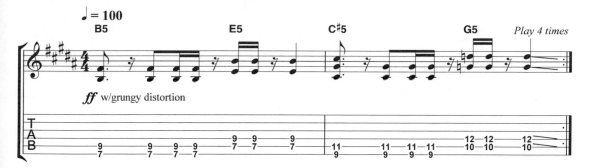

19 Power Slide

▼ Steve Vai

Barre chords

A **BARRE CHORD** is formed by placing your first finger across all six strings and then using the remaining three fingers to form typically an 'E', 'Em', 'E7', 'A', 'Am' or 'A7' shape next to it.

Barre chords can look very awkward in TAB form and beginners are apt to try to finger them using one finger for each note which can be tricky unless you mutate into something with six fingers! Here are some examples of common barre chords:

20 F

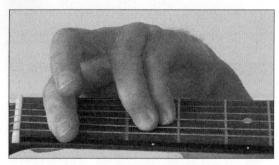
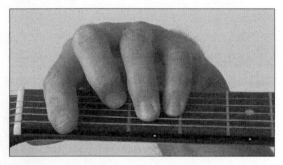

On the F chord, notice the three notes played at fret 1 – these are all held down with the index finger. The remaining three fingers form an 'E' shape.

Fm

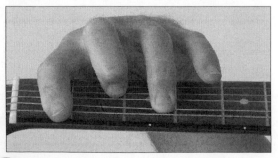
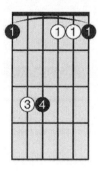

With the Fm chord, four notes are played at fret 1 suggesting that this should be a barre chord – notice that the remaining two notes form an 'Em' shape.

F7

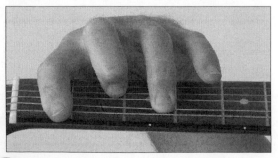
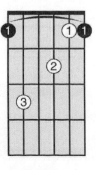

With the F7, an 'E7' shape is held down in front of the barre at the first fret.

21 B

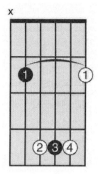

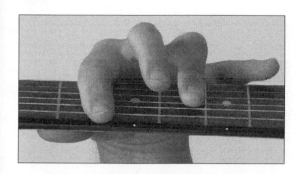

Bm

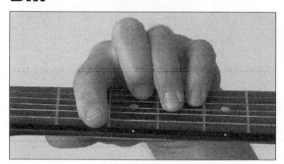

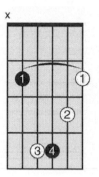

B7

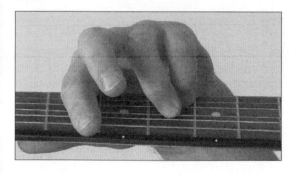

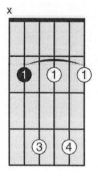

Get barred

When you see a suspect barre chord, pick out the lowest fret number in the chord.

Place your index finger at that fret and then see if the remaining numbers form a recognizable shape (usually a chord shape from the 'E' or 'A' family.

With a bit of practice you will soon spot barre chords a mile off!

These chords are all barred at the second fret.
The remaining fingers forming 'A', 'Am' and 'A7' shapes respectively.

▼ TAB for F chords

	F		Fm		F7	
T	1	1	1	1	1	1
A	1	1	1	1	1	1
B	2	2	1	1	2	2
	3	3	3	3	1	1
	3	3	3	3	3	3
	1	1	1	1	1	1

▼ TAB for B chords

	B		Bm		B7	
T	2	2	2	2	2	2
A	4	4	3	3	4	4
B	4	4	4	4	2	2
	4	4	4	4	4	4
	2	2	2	2	2	2

Basic Left Hand Techniques

22 Behind Barres

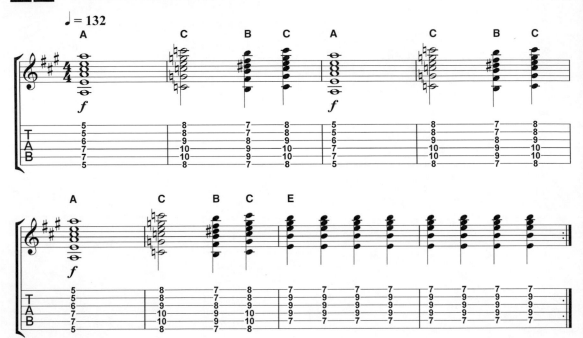

23 Minor Setback

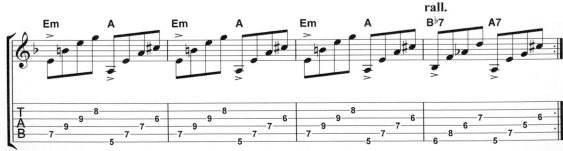

Left hand muting

MANY RHYTHM PARTS use a muted 'percussive' sound. Unless specified otherwise, the muting effect is best achieved by raising the left hand ever so slightly so that the strings come off the frets.

Left hand muting is shown using the 'x' symbol in place of a fret number on the TAB line.

Good muting technique takes plenty of practice to develop.

If this technique is new to you, start by playing the TAB very slowly and then gradually speed up.

Tip #8

Easier by ear

Many rhythm guitar figures use a combination of muted chords and chords that are fully sounded.

On the TAB this can look quite difficult to work out.

It is nearly always easier to get the exact feel from listening to the recording than to read it off the tab in close detail.

▼ PJ Harvey

Basic Left Hand Techniques

LEFT HAND MUTING is the key to playing great rhythm guitar.
Certain rhythm styles are almost impossible to play without it.

See if you can use muting technique to get a reggae feel on this next track:

24 Righteous Reggae

Slow reggae feel $\quad \downarrow = 90 \quad (\text{♫} = \text{♩.♩})$

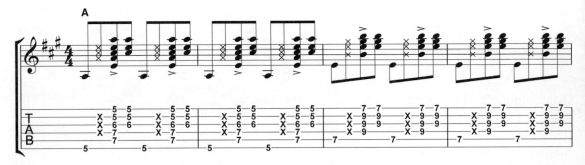

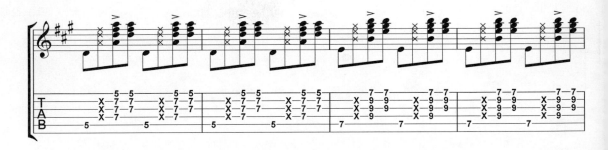

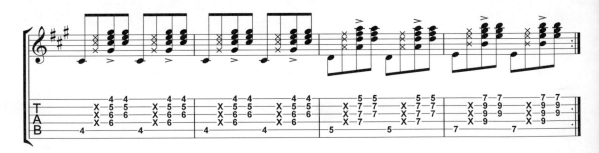

▶ Peter Tosh

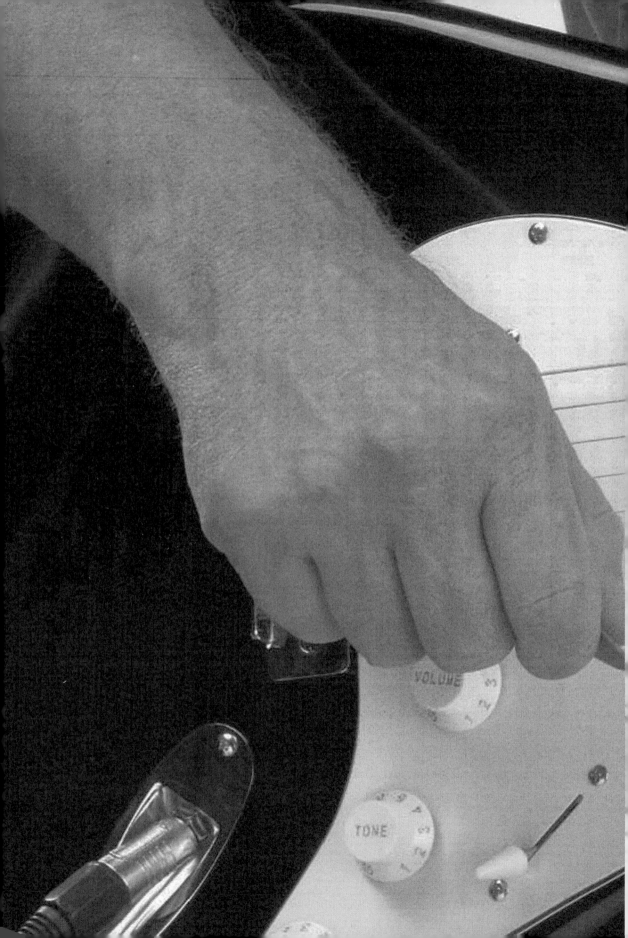

Basic Right Hand Techniques

Basic Right Hand* Techniques

*If you play guitar left handed then your right hand is the one at the end of your left arm!

Picking directions

SOMETIMES, particularly in books designed to teach you guitar technique, you will find picking directions marked.

The following symbols are in common use:

 Downstroke   V Upstroke

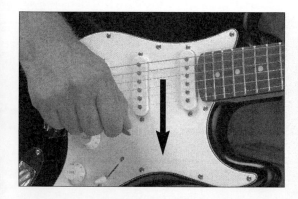
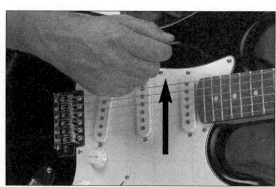

Tip #9

A sense of direction

Whether notated on the TAB or not, correct picking direction is often the key to getting the exact timing of a riff right.

For songs in 4/4 time try to figure out what the maximum number of notes to a bar is. It will usually be 8 or 16.

Use downstrokes on odd-numbered beats and upstrokes on even-numbered ones.

The following piece has a 16-beat feel.
The effect is achieved by a steady alternating right hand. The left hand damps the strings except where the chords are 'punched in' as shown on the tab.

Tip #8 'Easier by ear' (on page 25) applies!

25 Jungle Jam

Basic Right Hand Techniques

26 Minor Mystery

Slow and mysterious ♩. = 90

Fingerpicking directions

CONVENTIONALLY, fingerpicking patterns are shown by labelling the fingers of the right hand with letters corresponding to their names in Spanish.

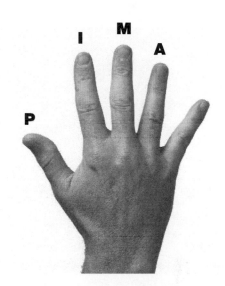

P (Pulgar = thumb)
I (Indice = index)
M (Medio = middle)
A (Anillo = ring)

Combinations of these letters sometimes appear below the TAB on songs that are best played fingerpicked.

For example, in the following arrangement of the old traditional folk song 'House of the Rising Sun', directions are given for the right hand fingerpicking pattern under the first line. The word 'simile' meaning 'continue in a similar fashion' is used to let you know that this pattern is then maintained throughout the rest of the song:

27 House Of The Rising Sun *(Traditional. arr. N. Minnion)*

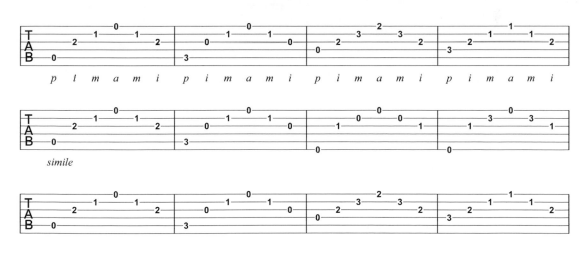

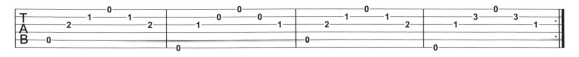

Basic Right Hand Techniques

All fingers and thumbs

Tip #10

In cases where no indication is given as to which fingerpicking pattern to use, you can usually work it out for yourself.

The basic rule is that the thumb looks after the notes on the bottom three strings, the top three being allocated as follows:

3rd (G) string — I (Index finger)
2nd (B) string — M (Middle finger)
1st (E) string — A (Ring finger)

The following song uses a distinctive fingerstyle technique that combines a pinch (two notes played simultanously with finger and thumb), an alternating bass-line and arpeggiated chords.

Follow the fingerpicking directions carefully to get the best results!

28 Farmyard Fingerpick

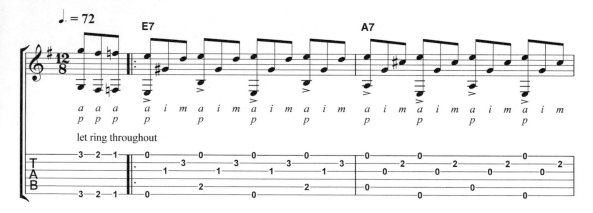

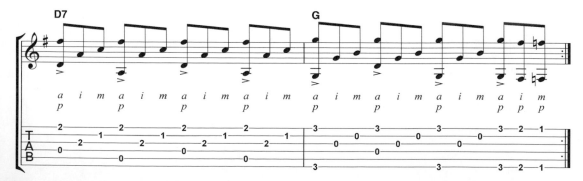

29 Sea Shanty Sprint

SOMETIMES the melody is carried by the thumb while the fingers keep up a rhythmic accompaniment using chord shapes:

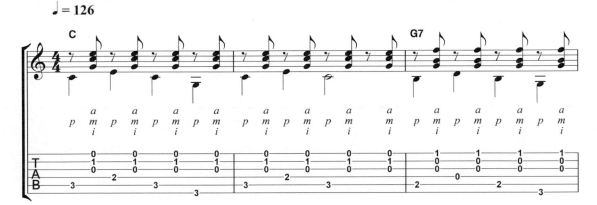

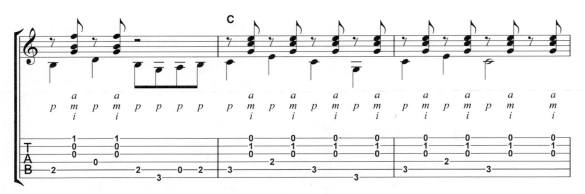

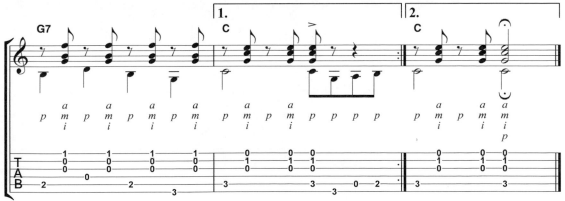

More Advanced Techniques

More Advanced Techniques

Harmonics

A HARMONIC IS produced by lightly touching a string with a left hand finger, precisely over a given fret (notably the 5th, 7th, 12th, 17th or 19th frets) while picking or plucking the string quite smartly with the right hand, to produce a clear, bell-like tone.

On TAB, harmonics are shown with the fret number enclosed in a diamond shape.

30
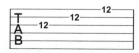

31 Hibernating Hedgehogs

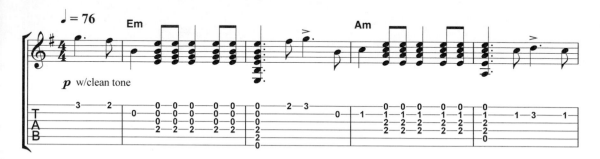

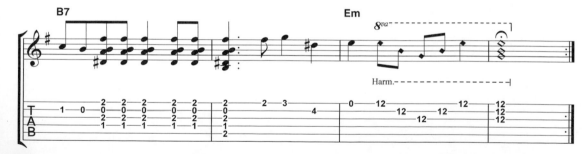

Palm Muting

THE LETTERS 'P.M.' are used to show passages of notes or chords that are played using palm muting.

To get this percussive effect, place the side of your
right hand against the strings near the bridge as you pick.

This effect is often used over extended passages of play,
in which case a dashed line (-------) shows you how long to maintain the effect.

More Advanced Techniques

32 Palm Muting Picnic

More Advanced Techniques

33 Shorty's Shuffle

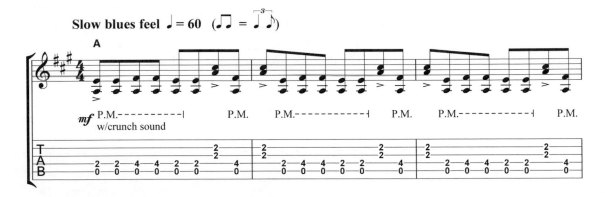

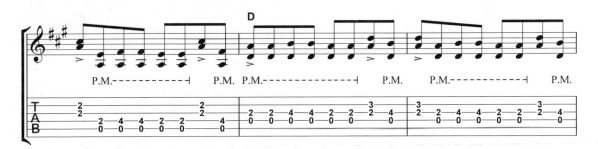

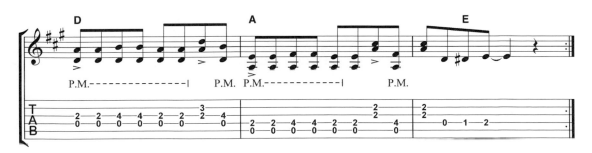

More Advanced Techniques

Bends

BENDING NOTES to change their pitch is fundamental to expressive guitar playing. But, because of the variety of technique used, this element is the one that most confuses new guitarists reading TAB. Let's take each type of bend one at a time and then look at how these combine to make up some of the best known blues-based guitar licks:

34 Decorative Bends

Sometimes called a 'Blues curl', a slight bend is often used for decorative effect.

In this case, the player is left to decide the exact degree of pitch change, but on the TAB it is shown as a ¼ tone bend.

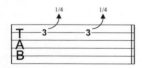

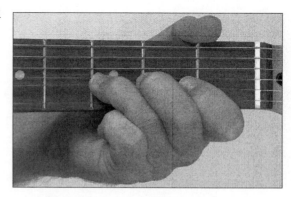

35 Bendy Blues

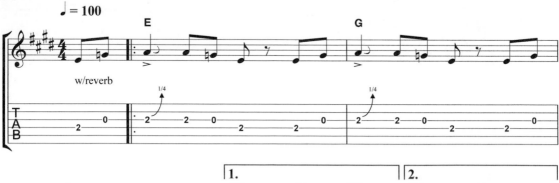

36 Specific Pitch Bends

HALF TONE and Full tone bends are played by bending the string so that the pitch shifts up by half a tone a full tone respectively.

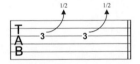

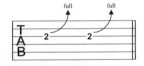

▲ **Half tone**

▲ **Full tone**

37 Pre-Bend

A PRE-BEND is where the string is bent before it is struck.
The bend is then released returning the pitch to normal for that note.
The result is a plaintive 'crying' effect.

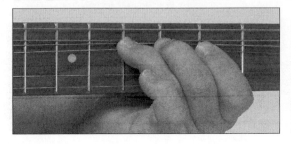

38 Bend And Release

HERE THE note is bent and held at the new pitch before being released back to its original pitch.

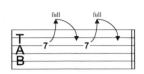

More Advanced Techniques

Achieving accuracy

To gauge the accuracy of a bend, use your ears to check:

For a half tone bend the note should sound the same as a note played one fret higher.

For a full tone bend the note should sound the same as a note played two frets higher.

39 Vibrato

TO SUSTAIN and 'sweeten' a note a string is fretted with a finger placed at right angles to the fretboard and the hand is then shaken to cause a rapid, but slight ,movement of the fingertip against the string. A wiggly line is used to show this technique on the TAB.

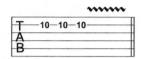

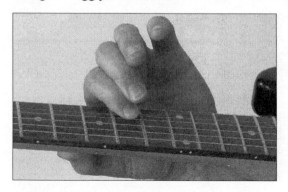
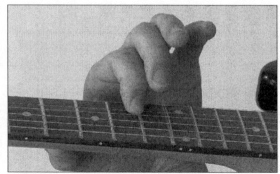

40 The Rake

THE RAKE IS set up by using the left hand to mute the notes marked 'x' on the tab and fretting the numbered notes so that they will sound clearly.

The marked strings are then played in ascending order with a rapid movement of the pick.

The rake is shown by a diagonal arrow on the TAB.

41 Country Curls

The following song demands a fine combination of bend and vibrato technique to get that melancholic (or should that be alcoholic?) country feel:

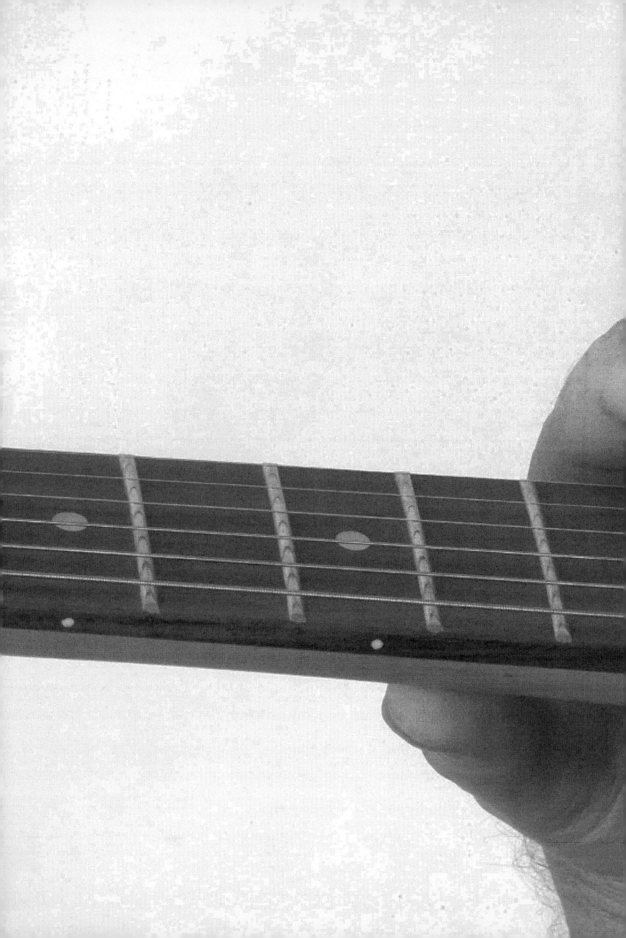

Putting It All Together

Putting It All Together

The most effective lead guitar solos are often those that are rich in different techniques and effects. At first glance, the TAB for these can appear the most daunting.

▼ Chuck Berry

50

42 Chucking It About

Here is my tribute to the great Chuck Berry.
My advice is to take Chuck's tune one chunk at a time!

Putting It All Together

43 Spaghetti Gunfight

FINALLY HERE IS a tune crammed with a variety of techniques.
It's inspired by those great Sergio Leone films that made Clint Eastwood famous.

See if you can use controlled bend and vibrato technique to get that eerie
'Spaghetti Western' feel. Remember to turn up the reverb!

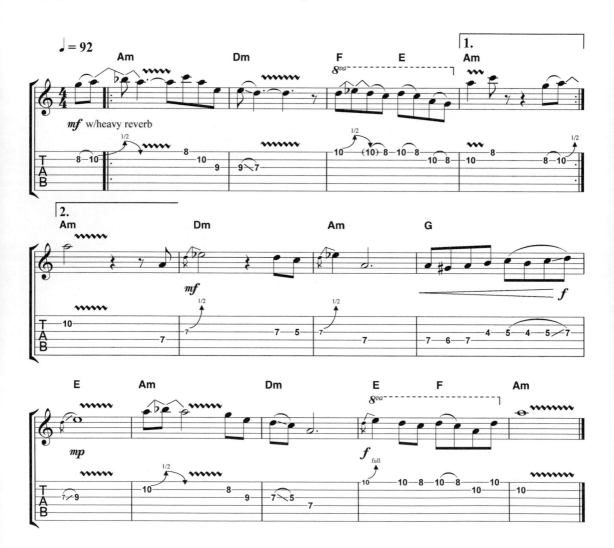

Notes on using a capo

TAB WRITTEN FOR songs that use a capo disregards the effect of the capo.

This means that, for example, a D major
shaped chord played with the capo at the
fifth fret would be written:

Even though, with the capo at the fifth fret these notes will actually be played at the 5th,
7th and 8th frets. So the fret numbers shown on the TAB are always relative to the position
of the capo.

Alternative tunings

All the TAB used so far in this book has assumed standard (EADGBE) tuning.
Non-standard tunings are usually clearly marked at the start of a piece of TAB.
For example:

'Dropped D tuning' (bottom E string retuned to D).
'Down tune half a tone' (all six strings tuned down a semitone).
'Tune to open G (DGDGBD)' (the notes in brackets tell you how to tune from sixth string
to first string).

Sometimes you will see a specific instruction like this:

1=D, 2=A, 3=G, 4=D, 5=A, 6=D

Tuning may also be indicated by markings
on each of the TAB lines at the beginning,
for example:

In this example the D chord would be heard as a D♭ because the guitar is tuned down
a semitone.

In all these cases you adjust your tuning at the outset and then read the TAB exactly
as you would in normal tuning.

Key to symbols

Repeat sign

'Repeat from' sign

Hammer-on

Pull-off

Slide

Legato slide

Decorative slide

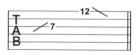

Muted (or percussive) notes

Picking direction indicators

 Downstroke

V Upstroke

Fingerpicking instructions for right hand

P (Pulgar = thumb)

I (Indice = index)

M (Medio = middle)

A (Anillo = ring)

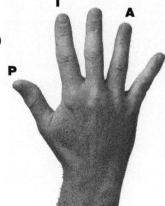

Harmonics

Palm muting

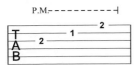

Decorative bend

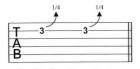

Half tone bend

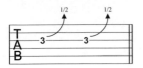

Full tone bend

Pre-bend

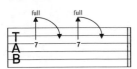

Bend and release

Vibrato

Rake